Anonymous

Life of James W. Jackson

The Alexandria hero, the slayer of Ellsworth, the first martyr in the cause

of southern independence. Vol. 1

Anonymous

Life of James W. Jackson
The Alexandria hero, the slayer of Ellsworth, the first martyr in the cause of southern independence. Vol. 1

ISBN/EAN: 9783337213824

Printed in Europe, USA, Canada, Australia, Japan

Cover: Foto ©Raphael Reischuk / pixelio.de

More available books at **www.hansebooks.com**

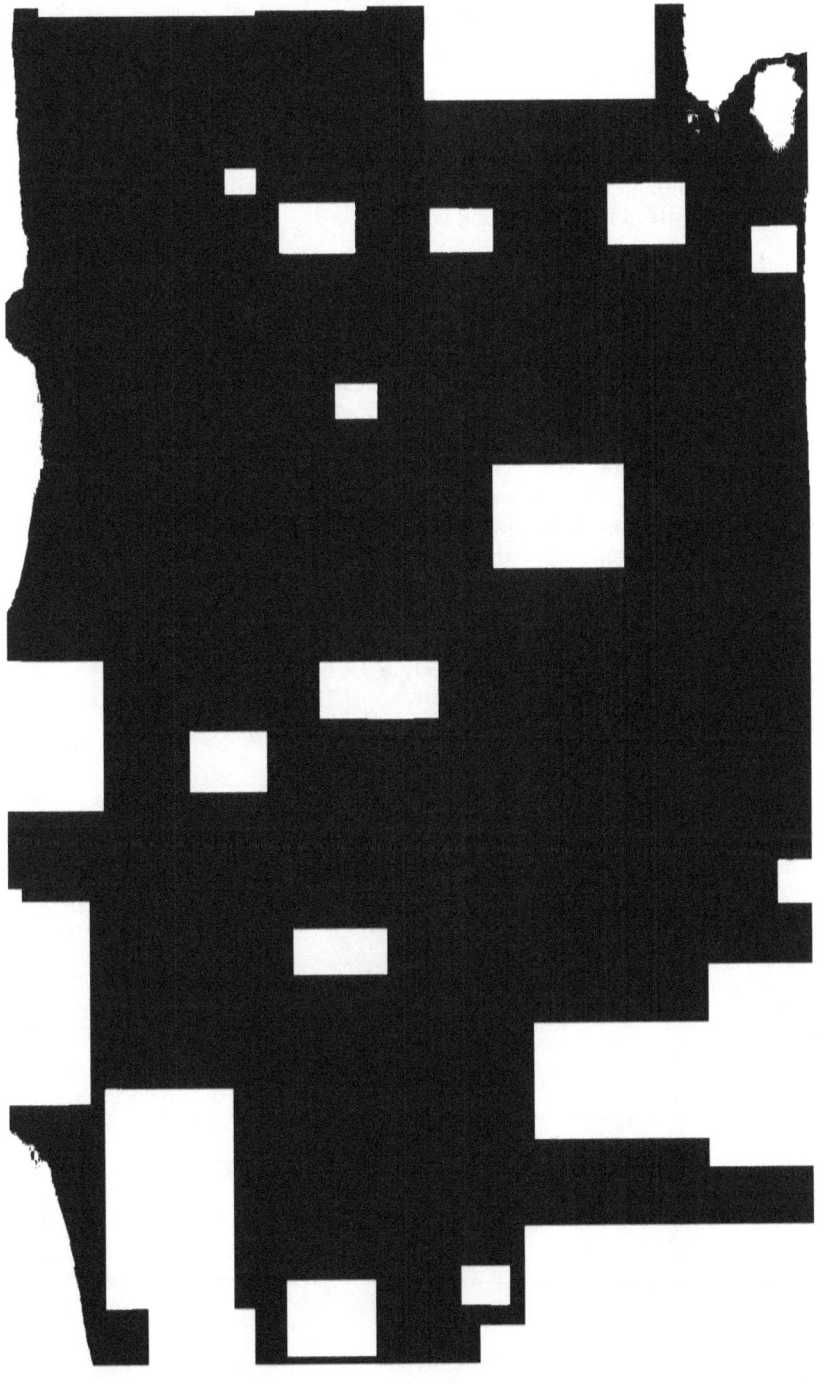

PREFATORY.

If any explanation may be necessary by the author of a work so eminently proper as this, of the hopes which have induced its publication, it is al' happily contained in the following letter:

VIRGINIA SENATE CHAMBER. *Feb'y 5th*, 1862.

CAPT. ———.

Dear Sir:

I have examined with care the manuscript of the life of my late brother-in-law, James W. Jackson, which you have submitted to me. I find that you have portrayed graphically and truthfully the many stirring incidents in his truly wonderful career.

Satisfied that the many acts of daring and self-sacrificing devotion to our holy cause which adorned the closing scenes of my brother's life will be, to our Southern youth, an inspiration to fire their zeal; trusting that the desire to know them, among our people, may prove of benefit to his stricken family, and convinced of its necessity as a matter of public history, I heartily approve of the publication of your work, and wish you every success.

Yours very truly,

HENRY W. THOMAS,

Representative 24th Senatorial District.

"Shout, shout his deed of glory,
  Tell it in song and story;
  Tell it where soldiers brave
  Rush fearless to their grave;
  Tell it—a magic spell
  In that great deed shall dwell."

LIFE OF JAMES W. JACKSON.

THE name of JAMES WILLIAM JACKSON is, perhaps, at this time, as widely celebrated throughout the Confederate and the United States, as that of any man, either living or dead. In the one country he is anathematized, villified and detested as the assassin of a gallant soldier: in the other he is lauded as a hero, loved for his devotion to the flag of his country, and the terrible determination with which he defended it, and glorified as the first martyr in the cause to which the blood of all her true sons is pledged. We will not discuss the question of their disagreement here, nor interrupt the regular course of our history by showing, (until the circumstances of the deed for which he suffered death shall themselves make it evident, in the order of their narration,) how utterly false and unjust is the light in which the North profess to regard that deed, and how absurd the application to it of the name of "assassination."

Certainly no man ever acquired *fame* more quickly than he, and certainly no achievement ever won it more desperately daring than his. Almost before his corpse was cold, the story of his triumph and his fall had thrilled through the land, on lightning wings, and he was cursed in Boston, Philadelphia and New York, as the unprincipled and mad destroyer of him who was the glory and boast of their chivalry, and bewept in Charleston, Montgomery and New Orleans, as the glorious and high-spirited type of Southern gallantry, prompt to avenge insulted honor, and ready to die rather than submit to the insolence of wanton and lawless invasion.

The circumstances were such as had not their parallel in history, and were invested with all the surroundings of interest that could bind to their contemplation the minds of men. A mighty political revolution was looming blackly up to the view.

A great nation was careening on the brink of a terrible precipice, and the breath hushed, and the heart beat quick in anticipation of the crash of the downfall which no arm could stay, save that of one man. He, not realizing his splendid opportunity, deaf to imploring entreaties, and blinded by his unholy lusts, saw not nor heard the premonitions of ruin. Two mighty peoples were sternly preparing their powers for the shock of battle, and the dreadful arbitrament of law. They were brothers, they had been friends; they were joint-tenants of a valuable property, their heritage from ancestors who had paid for its rescue from the misrule of tyranny, the priceless ransom of heroic blood.

But the one had forgotten their fathers' story, and wished to practice upon the other that very despotism which their all had been pledged to overthrow, and against which their solemn denunciations were hurled in life, and bequeathed in death. Envy of their brothers had possessed their hearts, and commencing, in revilings and cruel accusations, the exhibition of its rancor, had pursued its impious course through every labyrinth of injury, culminated in violence and bloodshed, and crowned its aggressions with threats of still more fearful significance even than the tenor of their fratricidal deeds. The other had warned them of the tendency of their course, and wearied out with the remonstrances of years, their hopes of a final cessation of strife and rendition of justice torn from them, one by one, they had demanded a division of their estate, and a settlement upon their separate patrimony.

But the stronger brother envied the richer fields and easy independence of the weaker, and refused to let him have the portion of goods that belonged to him. The latter warned, he remonstrated, he pleaded a peaceful separation. The treacherous brother pretended to grant it, and lulling him to security by promises of peace, improved the time granted to his professions, in preparing to compel a compliance with his wishes by force and fear. Then, when the mask was removed from the face of hypocrisy, and the last ray of hope had faded, a chivalrous people sternly and sadly prepared to win with the sword the rights which the exhortations of love had failed to secure them.

They commissioned their representatives to a common council, and through them, declared to the world that they were a separate people.

Still the other would not let them go. The vast power of the government, the army, the navy, a large numerical majority in population, every advantage were theirs, and they were confident of a speedy triumph over their despised foe. And now, while they are raising and organizing the army of invasion and subjugation, in the defenceless town of Alexandria, under the very guns of the powerful administration, the obscure and humble inn-keeper, Jackson, burning with detestation of the perfidious government, and with zeal and patriotic love of his new mother, raises over his home the chosen flag of his country, lies down to sleep under the protection of its folds, and pledges his life to uphold it from dishonor.

The invasion comes; the town is siezed; the small force—the advance guard of the gathering army of freedom—retiring before the overwhelming numbers of their foes, or captured by the perfidious violation of a flag of truce; blinded by his mad ambition, eager for distinction among the haughty invaders, a young and promising officer himself tears down the flag. Jackson is roused from his sleep by the noise of the profaning hosts: he hears their exulting cries as his beloved banner is ruthlessly torn down. Maddened by the insolence of the trespass, he rushes out to meet the violater of his house, and quenches in its life-blood the hate of the heart which had prompted it. Of course he is immediately sacrificed to the vengeance of his foes, and the victim of patriotism and the victim of tyranny fall, side by side, as their spirits rise to confront each other upon the eternal witness-stand.

The writer of this memoir knew Jackson well in all the relations he bore in life; in his public and private character; first when shortly after his marriage, the natural restlessness of his disposition had been temporarily subdued in the peaceful cultivation of a farm and the quiet delights of home, and since then, in his public life at Fairfax Court House and Alexandria. He was in Alexandria for several weeks preceding his death, and at the time it occurred, was *with him* until twelve o'clock on the night that ushered in so eventful a morrow, and enjoyed the mournful pleasure of visiting afterwards the scene of his triumphant fall and of gazing on the mute but pleading corpse. In preparing this tribute to his daring, this souvenir to his memory and the glory of his heroic death, he will not attempt any romantic coloring of his life; eventful and remarkable throughout, it does not need any. The friends who knew him not, but who thrill with admiration of his heriosm, must not expect to find in his character anything super-mortal—though his deeds may have partaken of that nature. The faults that he had, in common with us all, the true historian cannot extenuate. His many good traits shall be set forth without over-laudation, his life narrated us correctly as possible from the facts now able to be collected, that the reader who saw him not in the flesh may form a proper ideal of the life and character of the man.

In person, Jackson was tall and stout, at least six feet in height, and very powerfully framed. He was generally considered while he lived there, the strongest man, or least the best pugilist in his county (Fairfax), with, perhaps, one exception, a man of almost gigantic frame, named Peacock. His face was remarkable in its expression. Grim, stern, obstinate *determination* was stamped emphatically on every feature. The forehead was low, and on it the hair, always kept short, stood up defiantly. His brows were prominent, his eyes small and keen; he had high cheek-bones, an aquiline nose, and full and finely-turned lips and chin. His mouth was indicative of sensuality; but at the same time it heightened, by the firm compression of the lips, the distinguishing character of his face. When very young he must have been quite handsome, but at the time of his death, he being then thirty-five or forty, the features had become somewhat hardened, from the unsettled and violent life he had led. He was lithe and active, and his address graceful and pleasing. Those who knew him in early life will recollect the general affability and politeness of his bearing. He was then neat and comely in his dress, and his elegant figure made him indeed conspicuous.

Jackson's father was Richard Jackson of Fairfax. He married Jane Donaldson of Baltimore. They were very worthy and

highly respectable people. They had seven children. The eldest
daughter married Mr. Stewart of Fairfax, the second Dr. Evans
of Virginia, now dead, and the third Major Henry W. Thomas,
the present distinguished representative of the counties of Alexandria and Fairfax in the Senate of Virginia. His family now
reside in Richmond. John, the eldest son, is a physician of fine
talents, wealth and standing near Lebanon, Kentucky. In
November, 1861, he shot and killed one of a party of Yankees
who came to his house traspassing and insulting. For this,
when last heard of, he was in the jail of Lebanon awaiting his
trial. How forcibly does his deed remind us of that of his
heroic brother! The second brother, Richard, lives in Washington. Charles, the third, is in the 17th Regiment Virginia Volunteers, Col. Corse. James was the youngest child. The family mansion, a fine old country house, is on the Georgetown
and Leesburg turnpike, 8 miles from Georgetown. · The Post
Office was kept there in the old times of scarcity of houses
whence the one now used has the name of the house "Prospect
Hill." The boys were early distinguished for their bold and
restless dispositions. Especially so was James. Talents he had
of high order. His father died when he was but six months
old, but his mother did everything to secure her children the advantages of education. She was preparing to send him to the
Georgetown College, when, by the advice of his brother John
he was sent out to him in Kentucky and entered the Catholic
College in St. Louis. He did not stay long however, but re-
turning to Kentucky remained sometime there with his brother
who was very fond of him.

Had his talents been diligently improved he would have been
distinguished in some respect, for he had a fine judgment united
with great shrewdness. His mechanical turn was remarkable.
But he did not relish the dry details of study. He was fond of
the open air and the hardiest sports that manhood indulges in.
Indulging freely·the rude bent of his inclination, he became in-
volved in numerous hardy adventures, mostly *souyht* by him in
wanton love of the sport, and in the very exhuberance and over-
flow of strong animal courage, so that his name, when the writer
of this first heard it, was, in his neighborhood, a ·synonym of

athletic daring. This fact is not to be mentioned in blame. Many a life has commenced in the same way, and after having been crowned with usefulness, terminated most honorably. The old revolutionary hero Daniel Morgan was, in his youth, just such a man as James W. Jackson, the hero of the new revolution. Violent his nature certainly was, but it had not that violence that is the offspring of guilt. Had not the attendant and surrounding circumstances of his early life aided the development of this trait, or had some strong influence otherwise directed it, he *might* have been, with his talent and physical advantages, an ornament to the highest society, and "this deponent" can testify with pleasure, to many acts that show how kind and obliging a nature was his. Eminently social in his disposition he could not brook confinement or loneliness. He had always his house filled with company.

He bore in reality the character of which his face was so striking an indication. He was terrible to an enemy. He knew no fear on earth, nor any yielding from his resolution, but to those he loved he was devoted and true. He was a most zealous and self-sacrificing friend. As a landlord, which avocation his social impulses led him to adopt, he was studious to please and accommodating. Whenever in moments of passion or irritation he injured a friend or attacked without provocation, he was always most prompt to acknowledge his fault, as soon as an opportunity offered. The faults of such a nature are venial.

For one thing certainly his memory should be ever dear to all true sons of the South—his devotion to their cause. That indeed, was a solemn principle with him. He would brook no insult to his country, no breath of accusation. However high the position, however numerous the friends of him who uttered it, Jackson cared not—in that name would he smite though hosts stood arrayed against him. This was frequently illustrated during the exciting political tempest that agitated the whole country in the summer and fall of 1860, and the winter of '61. He was ever bold to denounce and prompt to punish any word even of apology for Abraham Lincoln and his insane party, however great the threatened detriment to his own interests in consequence.

But let us take up the story of his life and gather our opinion from the incidents with which it abounds. The early part of it was spent alternately with his mother in Fairfax and his brother John in Kentucky: There he became inured to those hardy sports and skilled in that rifle-practice which he so much loved. There he met and married Miss Susan Maria Adams, the daughter of a gentleman in Washington county, near Lebanon. She is a lady of the sweetest manners and appearance, and during their life together her gentle influence over him, fearless and obdurate to almost all else, was striking, while not the less so was his devotion to her.

He had been recommended to this lady and she to him, by a Catholic priest, her cousin, but a short while before their marriage. The priest, who had thought Jackson all along a zealous Catholic, reminded him of his "duties," and tried to bring him to the confessional. To this he demurred, and the reverend father changed his recommendation to objection, and tried to break off the match by slandering him to the lady's father. She, hearing of it, informed her lover. He married her, notwithstanding the priest's opposition and the coolness of the father occasioned by it.

When he was about starting to Virginia with his bride, he sent for the priest and questioned him in regard to the reports he had heard. He denied having spread them, and Jackson requested his written denial to show to his father-in-law, but the priest refused it. He then told him he would have to do that or take a thrashing. Finding he must fight, the holy man took off his gown and prepared himself for business. Jackson's first impetuous attack made him understand that he had plenty of it on hand; but he was a tough and hardy Kentuckian, and took blows and knocks as unflinchingly as old friar Tuck himself, and he gave Jackson a long and bloody battle. At length, however, the unexercised sinews of the priest began to tire, while the arm of the yeoman, hardened by practice in the work, still fell heavily. Jackson, desiring in the first place to punish his adversary, and rendered still more desirous of it by the tough resistance he met, now showered his blows fiercely and unmercifully, and gave the priest a most terrible beating. So severe was it, that the priest obtained a warrant and a posse and followed him to Louisville. There, however, he frightened the constables and all, and his faithful brother John coming to his assistance, he succeeded in escaping the wrath of the beaten ecclesiastic.

It was doubtless the gentle influence of his wife, whose refined and sweet disposition would make any home attractive, which, controlling his adventurous nature, kept him for several years free from the associations to which he had once been inclined, and induced him to settle down to the quiet life of a farmer. This he did, on his small farm near his mother's, in Fairfax.

"It was here," writes a young man of his county, who has furnished us with the account of several facts in his history, "that I first knew him. In the summer of 1854 I returned home finally from college, my father then living on a farm adjoining the one that Jackson cultivated. Among my 'acquisitions' at college was a rifle, won in a raffle, and as soon as I reached home I proceeded to try and acquire 'the hang' of it by practicing on the game which abounded in the neighborhood. I had been out many times, and though I had frequently had fine opportunities, yet, somehow, I did not succeed in killing anything. One day I had been out after squirrels, and having hunted for some hours, and fired several times without effect, I had lain down near a hollow tree to wait for something to show itself. There, reflecting on my lack of luck, and wondering whether I would ever make a backwoodsman, I fell into a sort of doze or dream, from which I was startled by the sharp crack of a rifle near me, followed by a heavy thump, as a large squirrel fell dead by my side. I jumped up, and beheld a man a few yards off quietly loading his piece.

"Did you kill that squirrel with a rifle?" I asked.

"Yes," he replied, "and I didn't *hit* him, either, if I shot true ; see if I did,"

I picked the squirrel up, and, sure enough, no bullet mark was on him.

"I came the Kentucky dodge over him that time," said he, now approaching, with a smile on his face at my perplexity.

"That's what we call barking," and he proceeded to explain

that he had shot so as to raise the bark upon which the animal was lying, and kill him by the concussion.

He then looked at my rifle, and I informed him of my inability to hit with it. Selecting a spot on a tree, about fifty yards off, he raised my piece and fired. His ball struck the *edge* of the tree, but directly on the horizontal line of the mark. He moved the sight a little, loaded and fired again, and this time his ball "plumbed the centre." ·

"Now," said he, "I think you can hit something. Come with me and try you luck."

I started, and soon found he was as expert at finding as in securing game. We presently had a shot at another squirrel, and in the course of a short time had secured four, one of which I had the extreme gratification of "bringing down" myself. I had told the stranger who I was, but did not know his name until he asked me to go by home with him, and pointed out his house as we emerged from the woods.

"Why, that is Jim Jackson's house," said I.

"Yes, and I am Jim Jackson," replied he, with a smile, as he observed a curious expression on my face, for I really was astonished to find that my kind and affable friend was the redoubtable knight-errant of his neighborhood.

"You've heard of me, I reckon," continued he.

"Yes, I have," I said.

He replied, "Yes, and you've heard a great many lies about me, too. There are some people in this neighborhood that pretend to think because I get into a frolic or a fight sometimes, that I'm a rascal," he said, and then he muttered, "I would like to trace some things I hear to their source."

I went on home with Jackson, and at his house I was introduced to his wife, and was much delighted with her quiet and attractive manners, and could not help thinking that a man must have much gentleness in him who could win the affections of so evidently refined and ladylike a person.

Jackson entertained me pleasantly, and before I left made me, with his own hands, a new ram-rod—mine being too short—and fixed my rifle in good shooting order. I departed much pleased with my visit, and we frequently hunted together after-

2

wards, and I had the gratification, under his tuition, to think myself soon quite an expert "backwoodsman," and to know I was a very fair rifle shot.

These trivial things are mentioned now in justice to the softer and finer traits of a disposition rough and unpolished, it is true, and on that account often hurried to the commission of acts which have sometimes received the censure of his acquaintances, which acts, most assuredly, his nature, in its moments of reflection, strongly condemned, whenever they were worthy of condemnation.

The reader of the previous pages can now have a very fair idea of Jackson's character. Let them reflect that his kindness to the writer of the preceding adventure was entirely without any hope of advantage, and must, indeed, have also been without any pleasure derived from it, except that of conferring pleasure, for he adds: "I was certainly not much company for him, and even less assistance than company, since it was seldom my skill contributed to the stock of the game; yet he nevertheless insisted always on an equal division, never hinting of a claim to the lion's share, to which he was justly entitled; neither would he ever visit my home with me, to partake of the bounty which his skill had furnished for my father's board, while I was frequently forced to accompany him to his own house."

His stay on the farm, which was altogether about four or five years, must have constituted the most happy part of his life, though, as it was also the most quiet, perhaps he did not think so. He yearned for more active, or at least more public life, and accordingly, in 1858 he leased the "Union Hotel," at Fairfax Court House, and established himself there as its landlord. Often, after the eventful scenes of the great storm had begun to appear, has he looked up at the old sign which used to swing before the door, and laughingly threatened to cut the "Union" from it. Had the letters been supposed to give an indication of his sentiments he would doubtless have done it, for he became very early a Secessionist. Whether anything was eventually done with it or not by him, we cannot say; but in April, 1861, when the Virginia troops were gathering together to defend their homes, the old board had ceased to swing. The wires

which held it were fluttering from their posts, but the board •
which once pointed out to the weary traveler a place of rest,
whether taken down by patriots unwilling to see its vain device
elevated among them, or swept down in their wrath by the winds
of heaven, was gone! Even with the Government, its distinction recalled, it was gone! And the beacon which had so long
pointed the weary traveler through the waste of life to a place of
rest and freedom, even as this old memorial of its name, was
gone, the ties that held it to its time-honored post rudely snapped
by tyranny's violent hand.

Pity it is that it could not have stood. When last we trod
the oppressed streets of Alexandria, the "gallant" Zouaves
were displaying their unexampled heroism in a perilous but suc-
cessful attempt at removing from the offended eye of the indignant public everything befouled with the epithet of "Southern."
The sign of the "Southern Protection Insurance Company" had
just been torn from its fastenings and precipitated from a second
story window into the thronged street below; that of the
"Southern Churchman" also had been torn off and demolished.
Whether the righteous indignation of our own soldiers would
have vented itself in like manner on that old sign-board, if it
had stood till they occupied the place, we know not; but we
wish it could have been left. It would have been a speaking
memento, though a very humble one, of the devotion a brave
people once had to a great Government, while the desolation it
would now mark, (for from that temple of justice on the one
side the dogs of war have chased her custodians, while our pickets shelter their horses in the portico of the hotel on the other,)
the determination of that people to tear from their hearts their
allegiance to that Government, now prostituted to the lust of
despotism, though desolation follow in the path of their attempt.

While Jackson kept this hotel, its run of custom was large.
He was attentive to the comfort of his guests, and his table was
well supplied. So far as his means and influence extended, he
endeavored to amuse and accommodate the public in the true
spirit of his craft. To accomplish this, he added a restaurant
to his hotel for the accommodation of appetites of all sizes, but
that part of the business did not pay, and was shortly aban-

• doned. Indulging his strong social feelings, he instituted a series of "hops" or entertainments at his house, and whenever he happened to encounter a good musician, he would call an impromptu "ball," and afford the young people of the village an opportunity of enjoying themselves together. He was always at the head of anything tending to public amusement, and in the tournaments, balls, &c., which flourished so during those times, he bore a leading part, if, indeed, he did not give the first impetus to them himself.

In the fall of 1859 was the John Brown demonstration at Harper's Ferry. The whole country knows the effect of that raid upon Virginia. Like the ready warriors of Clan-Alpine, at the shrill whistle of their chieftain sprang up the sons of the proud old Commonwealth, as that note of alarm pealed throughout her borders. We could almost realize the description of the poet:

> Wild as the scream of the curlew,
> From crag to crag the signal flew.
> Instant through copse and heath arose
> Bonnets and spears and bended bows;
> On right, on left, above, below,
> Sprang up at once the lurking foe;
> From shingles gray their lances start,
> The bracken bush sends forth the dart,
> The rushes and the willow wand
> Are bristling into axe and brand,
> And every tuft of broom gives life
> To plaided warrior armed for strife.

The Fairfax boys were not behind-hand in this respect. Among the first companies formed after the raid was the "Fairfax Riflemen," Capt. Wm. H. Dulany, and to this company Jackson at once attached himself. It is now of the 17th Regiment Virginia Volunteers, Col. M. D. Corse, and has done much service during the war, and was one of the few companies engaged in the battle of Bull Run, July 18th, when the Captain and several of the men were wounded. Jackson's brother, Charles, is now a member of this company. In it he continued till the winter of 1861, when, matters growing more serious every day, and it being plain that war was at hand, he, by strong exertions, succeeded in raising another company (of artillery) from the neighborhood, of which he was elected Captain. Removing to Alexandria shortly afterwards, he was not able fully to organize his men; but when the troops were ordered out in April, he summoned them to Alexandria, and kept those who assembled, amounting to about one-half of the company, at his own house for some time, when, from the rush of business in the town, he having to furnish meals to several companies besides, he being unable to bring them all together, he disbanded those he had. Whether the company would have been completely organized, had he lived, it is impossible to say; but those who know the indomitable spirit and determination of the man, will readily believe that he would have had it soon ready for gallant service.

While our troops were in Alexandria, Jackson was very urgent in his request to Col. Terrett to allow him twelve men to go with him to burn down the Long Bridge; but Col. T.'s instructions not allowing him to authorize such proceedings, it was not permitted. We can but think that if it had been done, it *might* have changed the state of things in the Alexandria neighborhood to the advantage of our people. Jackson went several times in the night to the bridge to see if any Yankee pickets had ventured across, but did not discover any. Once he went through Washington to spy out the indication of the enemy's movements.

Events of great significance began rapidly to crowd upon the stage after the Harper's Ferry affair. The fanatics at the North, whose unholy labors had brought upon the insane old man who headed that monstrous attempt the destruction that he had blindly rushed into, were not able to see, even in the bitter disappointment and failure of his effort, and the determined spirit it awakened in the South, an argument of the folly of their course. Instead of condemning his conduct, and striving to heal the bloody breach he had opened, they applauded his bravery, endorsed his act, and canonized his memory. Of course this only awakened the southern people to greater vigilance, while it sharpened their feelings against the poor old dupe that this fiendish fanaticism had driven to his doom.

Jackson had been one of the first to rush to Harper's Ferry, when the news of the raid spread through the State. Shouldering his tried rifle, which in his practised hands was so deadly a weapon, and mounting a swift horse, he started off. He did not arrive in time to use it however, nor to be "in at the death" with the marines, but reached these just as the assassins had been overpowered. He brought back with him one of the celebrated pikes, and a piece of flesh, which he said, either in jest or earnest, was part of the ear of John Brown, Jr., and from Jackson's humor it is very probable that it was so. These he exhibited for a long time at his house, and would detail with lively interest his conversation with old Brown, and the way in which he obtained his trophies.

The county of Fairfax was unfortunately at that time, as it had been for many years, infested with men disloyal to the vital interests of Virginia and the South. They had been received as brothers by the old citizens, and had settled there in large numbers, most of them professing a strong attachment to the cause of their adopted State, but the events of the past year have shown that, with only two or three honorable exceptions, they have proved false to their professions and recreant to their promises. Most of them had been very sly in their treason, or in uttering the sentiments they felt, but some had proclaimed their opinions with bold effrontery, and by their shameless conduct, brought difficulty and disquiet into some sections of the county. Now, however, they had to put a watch upon both acts and words, so that they might offend not in any way an aroused and indignant people. The true sons of the South now put forth every effort to detect and punish offenders. Foremost among the custodians of our rights in the county was James W. Jackson. No night was too inclement, no labor too severe to be braved, if an opportunity was offered to discover evidence against any man of offence against our already broken and battered laws.

During the spring of 1860, one Thomas Crux, his fanatical zeal overmastering even his Yankee cunning, was discovered to have been distributing the infamous Helper book and other incendiary documents, and uttering incendiary language. A watch was set upon him and proof of his guilt obtained. It was determined to arrest him, and Crux, feeling his guilt would be clearly proved, on his part determined to escape. His design was discovered by Joseph E. Monroe, a young man residing in his neighborhood, on the afternoon of the night which Cruz had set for his departure, and he as firmly resolved to prevent it. He applied to Jackson as the best man to aid him. Crux resided on the road from Fairfax Court House to Washington, about half way between the two places. The two proceeded towards his house in an open buggy as soon as they could get off, but when they arrived, they found the bird had flown. They resolved, however, to make the attempt to catch him, and so started on rapidly in pursuit. He had, however, gotten considerably the start, and it was not until they had reached the hill leading down to the Long Bridge, that they came in sight of him. He was riding in an open wagon with his son, and the night being a bright moon-light one, he recognised Munroe, and suspecting his object, at once put whip to his horses. The pursuers of course urged theirs on, and in a few minutes the old boards rang beneath the fiery gallop of their steeds, in spite of the prominent caution that stares the crossers in the face, threatening a heavy penalty to all who do not "walk their horses over the bridge." On they rushed, the pursuers right at the heels of the pursued, through the draw, over the planks, on to the causeway, on the Washington side. Here at last there was room to pass, and Munroe, heeding not the injunction to "keep to the right as the law directs," urged his swifter animal past the team of Crux, and pressed him against his horses while Jackson sprang from his buggy to the wagon, snatched the reins and stopped the team. Crux drew a pistol, but was afraid to use it against such determined courage, and found himself surely arrested for violation of Virginia laws, by a citizen, not an authorized officer, there within the jurisdiction of the abolition rulers of the corporation of Washington!

Still there was no way of getting off and he was taken by his energetic captors and delivered into the hands of the authorities. He was recognized to appear to answer the charges against him at court, giving bail in the sum of $2,500. When

the term arrived, however, the provident abolitionist, not relish-
ing a residence so far South as Richmond, knowing that proof
and confirmation strong of his guilt was surely to be forthcom-
ing, had made good his second effort to escape, leaving the
amount of his forfeited recognizance to the State. When the
circumstances of his capture were laid before the legislature of
Virginia they voted half of the money to the two men who had
taken him, as a reward of their fearless vigilance. Munroe,
though, did not live to receive his portion. He had a difficulty
shortly after this occurrence near Alexandria, with a man named
Howard, by whom he was shot and killed.

When Lincoln was nominated by the Black Republican party,
Jackson became a Secessionist and soon showed himself a ready
defender of his faith. Several times during the Summer he
wreaked a severe vengeance· on the partizans of Abolitionism
for proclaiming their sentiments in his hearing. It inflamed
him with fury to hear them proclaimed, and he would rush to
the defence of his cause as readily as to protect his own life.

The share he took in the cutting down of the Occoquan Lincoln
flag-pole showed how zealous he was. With characteristic insolence a party of miserable Black Republicans, some native, some
imported, had raised a flag sacred to Lincoln and Hamlin, at
at the town of Occoquan, in Prince William county.

Stung by the insult and by the further one of violence to a
young man who had fallen in with the flag-party and attempted
to argue against their act, having warned without effect, the
loyal citizens of the country determined to remove the flaunting
nuisance from the air it poisoned. They called a meeting for a
certain morning at Brentsville, the county town, a few miles
from Occoquan, of all those willing to assist in the work. There
was nothing to urge Jackson to go but his own feelings. He was
a citizen of another county, and Prince William affairs did not
concern him. But the affairs of *the South* concerned him, and
called forth all his fiery devotion. When the crowd marched to
Occoquan he was of it. The party marched into the town and
surrounded the pole. A Northern man then disputed with Jackson the honor of first sticking the axe into it, and after con-
tending for it good-naturedly a few minutes he accorded it to

him. Yankee stepped out, raised his axe, and then, his natural *instinct* suggesting it, turned around and inquired who was to bear the responsibility of his act.

"I'll take the responsibility of *this!*" thundered Jackson as siezing him by the collar he slung him around and sent him off with a kick. Then he grasped the axe himself and, with steady 'blow on blow,' soon brought the flag to the ground. He received the flag as his reward, rode into Fairfax Court House with it the next day, and long kept it at his house with his other Black Republican trophies.

Little thought the papers which chronicled this achievement that the same "stalwart yeoman" whom they then noticed, was in a few months to perform another deed the daring of which might eclipse anything outside of the pages of "romance or fairy fable," and which would place his humble name high up among the martyred ones in Fame's eternal temple. -

While narrating these exploits of Jackson, showing, as they do, the more violent traits of his character, it may be well, as it is certainly just, to tell of others which may evidence the softer ones ; and here a little episode, with which he was well acquainted, and every circumstance of which he knows to be true by the testimony of his own senses, strongly suggests itself to the writer of this memoir. When Jackson first commenced keeping the hotel at Fairfax Court House, he had employed as clerk an old Spaniard by the name of Arquilles. Where he picked him up no one knew, nor could anything of his former history be gathered from either of them. The old man was an excellent clerk, and managed the accounts of the house very satisfactorily ; but after awhile he began to drink rather too hard, so that his excesses brought on attacks which destroyed his usefulness and rendered him a burden rather than an assistance. For eight or nine months before Jackson's departure from the place he was an encumbrance to him, and was, during that time, supported by him. After his removal to Alexandria the old man became worse, and had one or two attacks of severe illness at the hotel where he was staying, being then kept by another man. He was, during his sickness, very unpleasant company, and his manners having been reserved and unprepossessing, had made no particular friends during his sojourn in the village. Jackson, however, who was with him when first attacked, notwithstanding he was then moving to Alexandria, and his presence was required there, remained with him until he was out of danger, and then hired men to stay with and nurse him. His sickness continuing, Jackson came from Alexandria to visit him, and finding he had been neglected in some respects, his anger against those with whom he had been thrown let itself out violently. He again hired attendance for him, and did not leave him till assured of his comfort.

The old man recovered from that attack, but fell back into his old habit, which soon brought on another. During all his sickness Jackson's attendance never ceased, he frequently leaving Alexandria (at a time when he must necessarily have been very busily employed,) to visit him, and when at last he died, Jackson had him decently buried. When we remember that this old stranger was poor, and friendless, and helpless, and that there was no tie at all to bind them, and no claim from one to the other except that of a short acquaintanceship, his course towards him is certainly deserving of praise, and his kindness of admiration.

We approach now, rapidly, the closing scenes of his life. It was some time in February, 1861, that he became "fixed" at the Marshall House, in Alexandria. The name of this house is now familiar as household words in the ears of two nations of people. It is comparatively a small hotel, on the southeast corner of King and Pitt streets. Many years ago, green among the boyhood memories of the writer, it was the finest hotel in Alexandria. It was then kept by one of the very princes of host-hood, A. G. Newton, now of the "Atlantic," in Norfolk. But in 18—, somewhere in the "forties," Mr. Green got ready his mammoth "Mansion House," and Mr. Newton transferred himself to it. Under his management, it of course became the chief hotel, and its diminutive rival, the Marshal House, went down. It went through the hands of several managers, but seemed to prove a bad speculation, as none of them cared to keep it for any length of time. At last it was purchased by Mr. A. S. Grigsby. From him Jackson leased it. Just before he took possession, it had undergone a thorough refitting—indeed, it was not completed till after he moved into it. Additions were made to it, and the old part of the house renovated, so that in May it stood an excellent house, well adapted for the quiet comfort of guests. And it was well patronized, for the events of those stirring times had flooded Alexandria with strangers from Washington, Maryland, and the South.

It was there that the "Washington Volunteers," a noble corps of young men, under the leadership of that chief of good fellows and genial gentleman, Major Cornelius Boyle, had their rendezvous. A battalion of companies already formed was also quartered there, and the commissariat not then having gotten under way, the troops were quartered in convenient buildings and fed at the hotels for some time after the establishment there of the military post.

Very soon after Jackson took possession of the house, he put up his flag. The staff was about forty feet long, and the flag a fine, large one. It was raised before the secession of Virginia as an indication of the sentiment of the man who slept beneath it. There waved its broad folds above the tops of the surrounding houses, visible from almost every part of the town, and plainly to be seen from the surrounding country, Washington, the Navy Yard, and the river. After the State had seceded, it then became not only the mere symbol of an opinion, but the proclamation of a faith, the emblem of a nationality, the tutelar protection of cherished rights. Flying, as it did, in the very face of the Government at Washington, it of course attracted the attention of the Northern public, and many a gallant editor, of the word-fighting school, waxed eloquent over the indignity, and lustily called upon the sons of thunder, with whom their ranks were *then* supposed to abound, to remove the foul insult from the offended sight of the majesty of Abraham Lincoln and Cabinet. No one, however, responded to the call.

There was published in some Northern paper, a few days after the taking of Alexandria, a "sensation" story about this flag, and an attempt to capture it by a daring Lincolnite. The account was gladly seized by the Northern press and published generally, and in all probability now constitutes among them one of the leading "legends" of this war. It was stated that a man, whose name was given, had gone to Alexandria for the purpose of taking the flag or perishing in the attempt. He put up at the Marshall House, and in the night quietly made his way to the roof and secured the object of his ambition, which he concealed by wrapping around his body and putting his clothes on over it. He met Jackson in the office, who simply remarked that he was a fat man (!). He then made his way to the suburbs, beyond which he succeeded in going, after accomplishing the very diminutive feat of knocking a sentinel down. He then went to a spot where an accomplice had promised to meet him, with the means of transporting himself and his precious burden beyond the reach of the "hungry rebels." He waited here for some time, but the faithless accessory failed to appear, and daylight beginning to make itself and himself visible, concluding he would certainly be missed and detected, he returned to the hotel and run the flag up again to its place, doubtless knocking down another sentinel on his return. Such is the story which was actually published at the North with the unblushing assurance of falsehood, claiming the credence of truth. Of course, it is abominably and outrageously false, but of a character, in every respect, with most of their publications—may we not say *all?*—bearing on the question now dividing our nations.

Jackson, of course, saw and heard what was written in regard to his flag. Indeed, it was a common joke to tell him that on such and such a day Master Abe was going to send some one down to lower his banner. Then it was that he would declare, generally with a smile, that "there would be two dead men about when that flag came down." Little did he think, perhaps, how soon and how literally his words would be verified. He also declared his intention to remain in Alexandria, and keep his flag waving under any circumstances.

Time wore on. The few troops stationed in Alexandria were expecting the enemy down upon them daily, but still he came not. On Thursday, the 23d of May, the vote was taken in Virginia on the Ordinance of Secession, passed in her Convention on the 16th of April. The city of Alexandria and the adjoining neighborhoods had given large majorities for the Union candidates at the February election. Whether the Federal Government waited purposely for the May vote or not, we do not know; but it is very likely they designedly delayed the seizure of Alexandria for fear of influencing the vote in the State. Such a motive would be in keeping with all their acts. But they little knew the spirit of the Virginia people, and fatally did they mistake the meaning of their former vote. The events that the tyrant's treacherous policy had since precipitated, had aroused the country to a sense of their danger and their duty. Alexandria and the neighboring districts gave large majorities in favor of the Ordinance of Secession—in fact, almost an unanimous vote for it.

Who, that bore a part in them, can ever forget the scenes that followed that day in Alexandria? Early in the evening—as soon as the result of the vote was finally known,—a party met to get up an "ovation" of some kind, to do honor to the spirit of the people, and to the members of the State Legislature who had been elected that day. Jackson was of the crowd—indeed one of the leaders. They determined to serenade the members elect. They accordingly procured a fine band, and when the proper hour approached proceeded to their houses, first to that of Mr. Cazenove, of the House of Delegates, where they were met and handsomely entertained by him, after having been received with a welcome uttered in burning words of patriotism. They then went to Mr. Thomas' house, State Senator, where they were thanked by a friend of his—he being absent. They then called on Col. Terrett, and were addressed by Col. Charles E. Stuart, in an eloquent speech, and having paid their respects to these "men of note," they played at the doors of several private houses, wherein dwelt the favored "divinities" of the party. The moon shone beautifully, the night was mild and balmy, the spirits of the people were light and free. Jackson was the guide of the band and entered into the pleasures of the occasion with all the eagerness of his disposition, taking the party to his house and crowning the festivities with a generous entertainment. At about 11 o'clock the party broke up and the music ceased. The happy companions of that night

parted. Who then guessed that of the eyes which then reflected
mutual enjoyment from each other, there were some which never
more should meet,'

> " Since upon night so sweet such awful morn could rise."

And now, save the sentinels who pace their solemn rounds,
the town is quiet, and the "all's well" that comes floating up
on the night breeze from the deck of the blockading and threatening vessel off the wharf, is distinctly heard. About one
o'clock the pickets from the long bridge gallop in, and report
the advance of the enemy to the cavalry officer in charge of the
outpost; he proceeds at once to Col. Terrett's quarters, arouses
him from sleep and informs him of it. His orders are immediately issued to the troops to prepare to march, and videttes
sent out to keep him advised of the approach of the enemy. A
little before day they have approached quite near, Col. Terrett
is just getting ready to retire, when an officer with a flag of
truce lands on the wharf and is conducted to his quarters. He
brings a demand for the surrender of the troops. This Col.
Terrett refuses, but signifies his willingness to evacuate the
town, and an agreement is made allowing him till 8 o'clock to
effect the evacuation, and the officer returns to his ship. Col.
Terrett at once puts his column in motion, and as his little force
marches out at one end of the town, the mighty thousands of
the enemy from the river and by the shore, march in at the
other. There is one fact that may be stated here, (thought not
bearing directly upon the subject of this memoir), to show the
perfidy of the foe. The agreement solemnly made under that
flag of truce *was broken*, and the company of cavalry ordered
by Col. Terrett to remain behind and give notice of any advance upon him, after 8 o'clock, was captured, notwithstanding
the protest of Capt. Ball against the violation of the compact.
Col. Terrett is now satisfied that it was but a *ruse* to capture all
his force, which the fortunate meeting with a train of cars just
outside of town, and the necessary delay in placing Capt. Ball's
company under guard, prevented them from accomplishing.*

---

* NOTE.—An officer of high standing in the Federal army has assured a
relation of his that *it was really designed* to entrap Col. Terrett and his

Col. Wilcox' assurance was given that it would be kept, and the excuse afterwards given was that it was an officer's private act. Shame on an officer who would remain in the service of a government which would force him to violate his faith! Eternal shame on a government which would adopt so paltry a subterfuge, to avoid an adherence to honor, as to attempt to throw the odium on an officer whose official acts honor should compel it to sustain. But they have more than once shown that to *interest*, with them, every honorable instinct is subservient. Alas, even for us who were once of them, that the United States government and the Unted States officers have proven so false to the instincts of honor, of gallantry, of humanity.

The main body of the force of six thousand, which achieved the glorious exploit of putting to flight four hundred men and capturing the town of Alexandria, came by land. The Zouaves, however, who had been encamped for some time in Prince George's county, Maryland, nearly opposite Alexandria, had embarked in steam-boats, and were landed on the Virginia side, some just above the town, others (comprising nearly all the regiment) at the wharves, with a large force of marines from the navy yard and the Pawnee. The landing took place just about, or a little after day-break. As a general thing the citizens were not aroused from their slumber, nor knew of the events going on for some time. Jackson was asleep at the time. The Marshall House was not in the direct line of march of either force, and the neighborhood was, consequently, not alarmed till the Zouaves had arrived there.

Some of the companies of the regiment had been sent off in diffierent directions, but the main body, under Ellsworth himself, formed at the wharf, and marched to King street, up which they filed in column of companies. Their appearance, as they

---

forces by this ruse of the flag of truce, and was laughed at in Washington as a good joke. Again: After Ball's company had been taken and placed under guard, the cavalry and artillery advanced after our infantry, and a lady whose husband is now in Richmond, from her residence saw them, on arriving at the railroad, unlimber their cannon to fire at the retreating train, which turned into the woods just in time to escape them. This is all true.

marched up the street, must have been very fine. Their fan-
tastic dress, the gleam of their sword-bayonets, the investment
of terror with which the braggadocio of the North had clothed
them, all conspired to make them as they came up on the double quick, an omen of direful presage. They had been peculiar-
ly the recipients of that *praise of anticipation* with which the
North has so liberally fed its soldiers. Together with that other
set, raked up by Billy Wilson from the cespools of infamy in
New York, they were held up to the eyes of the South as most-
to-be-dreaded soldiers, and terrible were the deeds predicted, if
once their " ungovernable heroic fire" should break out amid
the chaff of armed rebellion. Had the stories of Manassas and
of Santa Rosa Island then been written, they might have robbed the Zouave character of a portion of its terror, even as the
reception of Ellsworth and his "pets" in Alexandria must
have removed from the Northern mind a portion of its blindness.

On came the Zouaves up King street. Arriving at the Tele-
graph office, Ellsworth first captured it and placed it under
guard. As he came out of the door, his eye fell on the flag of
Jackson, flying from its pole on the other side of the street.

"Boys that flag must come down," he cries, and dashes up
the street. We are not exactly familiar with Zouave disciplire,
nor do we understand by what orders he effected the halting of
his men below, and the detailing of two or three to go with and
assist him in capturing "the prize," as he considered it, but it
was done. He walked or *ran* into the house and boldly demanded to be shown the way to the roof. The servants had
shrunk away and the clerk and a few gentlemen in the office not
answering him, they proceeded themselves to find it. Mounting
the roof, he assisted in hauling down the flag, while his admiring minions below gazed up with rapture at the scene.

It was at this time that Jackson was aroused. There is a
story that he was awake before, and met Ellsworth as he was
going up, and finding out his object, had then returned to his
chamber and procured his gun.* But whether this be so or not,

---

* See Appendix No. 1.

we know that he was suddenly roused from sleep, to find that his house was overrun by insolent trespassers. He hurried on a portion only of his dress, not taking time to put on his coat or shoes. He hears the noise made in ascending the stair, the trampling on the roof, and he knows what is going on. He remembers with what a sacred determination he raised his flag, and the aggravating manner of the insult to it appeals loudly to him to vindicate it, and he seizes his gun.

He knew—he *must* have known—the danger, the desperate peril of the attempt the idea of which flashed across his senses, and he may have hesitated a moment, but it was *only* a moment. Honor, faith, feeling, all were enlisted, and his mind was made up. To determine with him was to perform. He rushes by the nearest way to the main stair. He reaches the second story landing. Just as he does so, Ellsworth and his friends are descending the steps to the landing. Brownell in front. Ellsworth has commenced to wrap the flag around him, and remarks, as he receives it from one of the men, "I'll take the prize."

"Yes, and here is another for you!" rings the determined voice of Jackson, and his stalwart form confronts the despoilers. He presents his gun at Brownell, the foremost one, when suddenly his eye catches sight of the flag around Ellsworth, and with terrible energy he changes his aim to him. In vain does Brownell attempt to strike up the gun. Quick as lightning, Jackson brings it down, the fear-strung nerves of the Zouave not availing against his desperate resolve, and in another instant Ellsworth's heart receives the contents of one barrel. Then he turns with fiercer fury on Brownell, but the Zouave has already aimed his piece, and as Jackson is pulling the second trigger he receives the dreadful Minie ball through his head, and as he falls the other load is discharged from his piece, taking effect in the frame of the door on the sill of which Ellsworth has dropped. All was over in a few seconds, and while the Zouaves below are looking for the appearance of their chief and his trophy, the surgeon of the regiment rushes out, and informs them that their Colonel had just been "brutally assassinated!"

For awhile all is confusion around, the men being uncertain what to do, in so sudden an emergency. At length, however,

3

Ellsworth's body is raised and wrapped in a red blanket, a door is torn from its hinges, on which it is laid out ; running muskets underneath this, it is thus carried slowly and sorrowfully back, down the street up which, a few minutes before, he had so proudly marched.

The body was laid out in state at the Navy-Yard that day ; on the following, it was taken to the White House. When President Lincoln beheld the features of his beloved protege sealed in death, he is said to have wept bitterly. Abraham Lincoln weep! Far be it from us to offend against one of the finest instincts of humanity, by scoffing at the exhibition of even womanish weakness, in the man who is gazing on the mutilated remains of what has been a solace and a cherished love ; but tears from the man who can coolly jest at misery, as he heaps oppression on innocence, and condemn millions to unhappiness, to subserve the lust of one—*tears from him!* We confess the picture is a mournful farce to our contemplation. The corpse was conveyed from the White House to the depot, with ceremonial pomp, some of the features of which might have excited the envy of a savage, and which never would have been tolerated within the confines of civilization; but for the inhuman hate which prompted them thus to stoop in order to raise the vulgar sympathy of wretches in the cause of the despot. We allude to the exhibition in the procession, of the now celebrated flag, bloody and tattered, which was borne, immediately behind the hearse, by Brownell, on the point of the bayonet with which he had pierced Jackson's body as he fell.* This barbarous ceremonial was repeated in New York, on the arrival of the corpse there, which, having feasted the depraved appetites of the "b'hoys," and excited the vengeance of the "patriots," was finally borne to its last resting-place.

Of course the public mind, both North and South, was much excited by this extraordinary deed, and its mention was on every lip, of the one party to extol, of the other to condemn. The North, wonder-stricken at their manner, and maddened by the fact of their great loss, heaped all sorts of condemnation

---

* See Appendix No. 2.

on " the assassin of Ellsworth." We need only calmly survey
the *facts* to be convinced of the injustice of such an epithet
being applied to our hero. In the first place, in any view they
may choose to take of our position, whether they regard us as
rebels or belligerants, that flag was entitled to treatment and to
respect which it did not receive at Ellsworth's hands. If we
were to be regarded as belligerants, as an established Nationality,
even then the flag of his country, floating above a man's house,
in a conquered city, at an hour when the owner was asleep, and
had not had time to lower it, had a claim for respect good in
civilized and humane warfare ; even then, knowing, as Ellsworth
did, that it was a *private* affair, not marking or intended to mark
a spot to the defence of which its colors might direct its defen-
ders, but merely unfurled as an individual gratification, his gen-
tlemanly instincts, if he had them; his chivalry, if he possessed
what they claim for him, would have prompted him to pass it by
for another time ; or if his sense of public duty and public policy required it, to demand its removal in terms which might
have spared the feelings of its owner.

But affecting to regard us as "rebels," then the flag was a
mere indication of an opinion, openly proclaimed—under a sanction secured by the strongest guarantees, and to deny which
would be to establish the most offensive of all tyrannies. It is
the boast of the English and American law that however humble it may be, a man's house is his castle ; that though the rain
and the snow may enter it, nor King nor President may without
warrant of law. How easy would it have been for Ellsworth to
have summoned the proprietor of the house, and in proper manner and form, demanded and obtained a removal of the flag.
But ah, when once a man has stooped to be the tool of despotism, how soon is he accomplished in its dirty work ! Even so
with him. The *heart* had become tainted, and with its corrup-
tion was all the conduct infected. His whole course showed how
completely he was carried away, by his headlong passion, from
the path of reason. We can honor the hero who, in the storm
of battle, seeing the banner of his foe waving above a redoubt,
whence destruction is showered on his own ranks, gives utter-
ance to the gallant resolve, "That flag must come down," and

bravely leads his men to the attack. Ellsworth's resolution had in it nothing to claim our praise. Here was no battle, no resistance, nothing but the avowal of an opinion, by a brave man, not afraid to declare it openly, and which he had as much right to avow in the light in which Ellsworth professed to regard things, as Ellsworth himself had, eight months before, to run up the name of his master Abraham at his own mast head.

No, his achievement was not the military manœuvre of an officer, only anxious to discharge his duty with credit to himself and his cause, but the rash trespass of an invader, forgetting, in the blindness of selfish passion, what was due even to his own position. That flag had been somewhat marked, or if he was ignorant of that, it was the first "rebel banner" he had seen, and in the zeal of his selfishness, ambitious that *he himself* should be *the first* to achieve the *honor* of capturing a secession flag, (whether gallantly in battle, or from the roof of an over-powered private citizen, one among a thousand, would make no difference in the Northern idea of chivalry,) he rushed to the work himself. Dignified commander! Why did he not speak but the word to his intrepid Zouaves, that would have sped them from pavement to window, from window to roof, and in a jiffy have brought the unholy emblem of depravity to the earth? It would have been fun to them, and afforded a subject for their illustrated journals to embellish their pages with for weeks. How vividly would they have portrayed the daring ascent of the mountebank, up the walls, and the mute astonishment of the gaping Alexandrians below! But he must give them something better than that—*for him!* He must give them *his own* picture taking down that flag, and covered with the exceeding great reward of his daring. His whole course shows how completely selfish his intention was, and his taking the flag from the man who had it at first, with the exclamation. "I'll carry the prize," is an explanation of it all. Had he succeeded—had he gotten out safely—had he escaped the wrath of his one opponent—had he taken that flag to the White House and laid it before the admiring eyes of President and Cabinet, where would have been the praise, where the honor of the achievement? Doubtless it *would* have been among a people who herald as gallant actions the capture of unarmed men and helpless women, and the demolition by the fire of war of the peaceful citizen's home, and send up a voice of boasting triumph, as a hundred perchance may fall back before the onset of a myriad.

Looking at this affair as we ought, where is the right to apply the epithet "assassination" to Jackson's deed? The assassin does not confront his victim, when, armed and attended, he goes forth to conquer and to triumph. He does not give him warning of the blow he means to strike. No, he follows his footsteps stealthily, he seeks him out when alone, unarmed, and most unsuspicious of danger; he lurks, himself, in some hidden and secure corner, and from his hiding place leaping a moment, to strike, he hastily retreats, and seeks security in flight when his deed is done. Not so the Alexandria hero. He is aroused from sleep with the report that his city is invaded, that his home is threatened. He hurries from his chamber to find that that home has been forcibly entered. Being not a military barrack, being not the property of a government or corporation, he being peacefully engaged in it in his daily avocation, he cannot see the propriety of armed men violently entering it, under no warrant of law, or sanction of justice. And for what do they come? Not to arrest an offender, not to capture a fugitive, not to secure a prisoner, but to steal from him a portion of his private property. Has he not a right, by all law, to prevent such desecration, even, if necessary, by taking the life of the trespasser? And of what is it their intention to rob him? Of that which is as dear to him as his gold, as dear as any of his property, aye, as the honor of his family, and as life itself. He rushes to meet the soldiers; he finds them with the stolen property in possession, and in the fury of his offended manhood, he slays the chief of them. Alas! they were too many for him, and his life-blood might not ransom from their profaning hands the symbol of his faith, but he died as a man should die, in the defence of it. Let them attempt to color this affair as they may, they cannot deprive Truth of its power, and robbery is robbery, whether committed by the wretch, who relies for his protection on the darkness of midnight, and the silence of stealth, or by the marauder who overawes by armed battalions.

As if designed by heaven, the circumstances of this deed, the first invasion of our soil by our haughty foes, was to teach them a terrible lesson of the consequences they might expect. Ellsworth, proud, insulting, confident, violent, *invading forcibly* the house of a citizen who desired only peace in the possession of his rights, exhibited a true type of the Northern Government and character, and the deed of Jackson must have been a vivid indication to them of the determination of the South—a determination thousands of their best soldiers have since realized in dust and mortal agony—to die in their chosen tracks, to die on their violated soil, rather than submit to their invasion and spoliation.

After the double deed was done, the body of Jackson lay for some time upon the landing, where it had fallen. His wife, hearing the noise of the guns, had rushed out, to find her husband a corpse, but was forced back to her room, and a guard placed in the house, every door sentineled, for fear of some other onset by one of what the Zouaves had now learned to consider the "fiery" rebels.* A Confederate officer, who lodged that night at the Marshall House, being awakened by the reports, started to leave his room, to see what was the matter, when he was suddenly confronted by a soldier, who, with his musket presented at him, ordered him back. He recognized the Zouave uniform, and at once comprehending the state of things, went back to his room, where, having fortunately a suit of citizen's clothes, he succeeded in making his escape after the guard was removed. This was not done for several hours, and then the friends of Jackson were permitted to carry the body into a room and prepare it for burial. He was dressed in the uniform he had worn as Captain of artillery. There, as he lay cold in death, his face disfigured frightfully by the powder and the fearful Minie ball, his tall form robed in the suit he had donned for service in the ranks of his countrymen in their struggle against the power of despotism, with the balmy air of May floating in through the open window, what a scene it presented! What a stern and sullen calmness on the faces of those who laid out the dead! And the dead man's face! how resolute was its expres-

---

* See Appendix, Note No. 3.

sion ! how defiantly stood up the hair, and how terrible a triumph
sat in the firm compression of the pallid lips!

An old gentleman was busy cutting off locks of hair. and
wrapping them up. "Ah," he muttered, "let this be remem-
bered as coming from the head of the first man who shed his
blood in the cause of our Southern independence." And out in
the solemn streets there were groups of citizens with menace
lurking in their eyes, and soldiers gazing curiously at the house
of death, and a cloud was on every face and a chilled feeling in
every heart, that even the warm, genial sunshine of May could
not clear away. And so began the war of subjugation !

The next day the body of Jackson was removed from Alexandria to be buried, the family leaving with it. He left, besides
his wife, three little children, daughters, the eldest about twelve
years old.* They are children of exceedingly attractive appearance and interesting manners. Thus was the Marshal House
left behind. It was taken possession of by the Federal officers,
and the office used by the Provost Marshal. The house at once
became a scene of attraction for Northern soldiers and newspaper correspondents, who, wishing to have each a memento of
Ellsworth, began to chip off the railing and cut up the floor of
the landing where he had fallen. That being demolished—entirely *cut away*—they attacked indiscriminately the whole house
and furniture. Some of the citizens tried to save the furniture
by packing it all in one room, but the officers would not protect
it, and on the 7th of June, house, furniture, and all were one
common ruin.

The body was carried first to Fairfax Court House, and thence
to the old homestead, on the Georgetown and Leesburg turnpike, where it was interred. Whether it has been suffered there
to rest in peace, even thus far, we cannot tell. For a long time
the old lady, the widowed mother of Jackson, has lived there
alone. During the time when our forces held possession of Ma-
son and Munson's Hills, and their advanced pickets were within
a short distance of the Chain Bridge, we happened one day, with
a small scouting party, to halt at one of our posts (Lewinsville,)

---

* See Appendix, Note No. 4.

to regale ourselves with some excellent peaches, which our "boys" had procured from the neighboring orchard of an absconded Yankee. While there, Mrs. Jackson came up in her carriage, accompanied only by a small negro boy, her driver, on her way from her own house, which was outside of our lines, to her daughter's, Mrs. Stewart's, which was within them. The old lady had no pass, and was of course halted by the picket, the orders being at that time very strict in regard to permitting persons to · pass. Recognizing her, and divining whither she wished to go, we informed the Lieutenant in command of the post who she was, and to whose house we supposed she desired to ride.

"Jim Jackson's mother!" he exclaimed. "Sergeant, let her pass," and added, as he turned round to us, "if it costs me my commission."

Whether the old lady has been permitted the peaceful possession of her home since the Yankees extended the lines of their *protection* (*!*) around it, we cannot tell.* The torch has been ruthlessly applied to many a lately peaceful and happy home in that neighborhood, and it may be that this, for the sake of the associations that encircle it, has met the same fate, leaving but the "blackness of ashes to mark where it stood." We should not be surprised to learn it. And that old mother may now be an outcast and a wanderer, as many are. The hand of violence may not even have permitted the frame of Jackson to remain in the sepulchre wherein we saw him "quietly inurned." Their vandalism may easily have extended thus far. The spirit which prompted the destruction of the Marshall · House for the manufacture of mementoes, would probably exult in the procuration of the hero's bones as trophies, and the earth, which once struck awe into their hearts, may be condemned, in retaliation for the icy terror with which it once inspired them, hereafter "to patch a hole to expel the winter's flaw" in the hut of some Northern soldier who shall have retired upon such laurels, or the bones which formed that stalwart frame for Yankee children to "play at loggats with." Little can their malice harm him now! His fame is won, his glory is fixed, it cannot be shaken. Tyranny has done her worst with him. The first vic-

* See Appendix, Note No. 5.

tim to its lust, the first martyr to independence, he met, without fear or faltering, the death which, with him, was preferable far to the shame of suffering interference with his sacred rights.

When the cause for which he died has triumphed, when the insolent invaders shall have been driven from the sanctuaries they profane, or made to wash out with their blood their "foul footsteps' pollution," when we shall have fully shaken off the fetters which an impious and inhuman tyranny would throw around us, when the exiles shall return and repossess their own, and the walls of our temples be rebuilt, then will a mindful nation erect over his remains, if they be found, in their sacred places if they be not, testimonials which shall speak to the traveller and guest the admiration and respect which his heroic deed and death has inspired for his memory in the hearts of his countrymen.*

Who can doubt the speedy triumph of chivalry, gallantry, and resolution over treachery, inhumanity, and despotism ? May God defend and prosper the right !

---

* See Appendix, Note No. 6.

APPENDIX.

Note No. 1—Page 32.—There have been several different versions of the circumstances immediately preceding the killing of Ellsworth, but the one we have given is the true story. Mr. Alexander, the clerk, was asked by Ellsworth, when his party entered the house, the way to the flag, but gave no answer, and they passing on, he immediately sent word to Jackson by a negro woman, to come to him directly. Jackson was going without his gun, when the woman mentioned that the house was full of soldiers, who did not look like our soldiers, and this remark caused him to take it. She begged him to leave it behind, and he ordered her to cease her entreaties, adding very sternly, "Don't say one word about this to Maria,"—(his wife.) He then went to the office, and thence up the steps, meeting the party as related.

To show the daring resolution of the man, we mention another fact, which we only recently learned. He had obtained a small four-pounder cannon from some friends in Alexandria, the one used there almost from time immemorial to fire 4th of July salutes with. We had frequently seen it in the back yard of his house, behind a screen, pointing to the front, but knew not until lately informed, by a distinguished officer in the 17th Virginia Regiment, (whom Jackson had confidently told,) that it was loaded almost to the muzzle, and that he had gotten Capt. Kemper, of the artillery, to aim it so as to rake the passage to the office, the office itself and the front entrance, for the purpose of discharging it when the place should be thronged with Yankees, in case they should enter his house. The officer, when told of this, remonstrated with him on the desperateness of this resolution, as he would most certainly be killed for it. "Well," he replied, "I have not a long time to live anyhow, and if I can kill fifteen or twenty Yankees, I'll be willing to die."

Doubtless, had it not been for the suddenness of the information, and his being asleep at the time, he would have sold his life more dearly than he did, as the effects that Vienna and Manassas witnessed of Capt. Kemper's splendid aiming give us every reason to suppose that Jackson's cannon was well directed.

Note No. 2—Page 34.—We have heard nothing lately of Brownell, whom accident placed for a while among the Northern rabble on the throne of a demigod. A gentleman who saw him afterwards in Washington, describes him as most ordinary in his appearance, and the true type of a New York *sub-life-boy*. He wore then, over his uniform jacket, a rough, black over-coat, had his pants turned up, and a white felt hat cocked on one side of his head. He talked in a sing-song way, had a down-cast look, and when he opened his mouth to roll over the stump of the cigar he held in it, you could perceive that several of his front teeth were gone. He was at that time flourishing proudly the silver-mounted pistol which the merchants of New York had presented him as a reward of his "gallant action!"

We state in this connection the report that Jackson's flag could be seen from the White House, and that Ellsworth had promised Mrs. Lincoln to present her with it on the evening of the 24th of May, which we have every reason to believe to be true. We omitted to mention the fact of Jackson having taken down his flag to add a new star as each succeeding State seceded, and the wildness of delight with which he lowered it, and cut out with his own hands the large central star when Virginia took her stand with her Southern sisters.

Note No. 3—Page 38.—The barbarity displayed towards the dead body and the cruelty to the living friends of Jackson by the Zouaves, is really shocking. The body was pinned to the floor by a bayonet, and no friend allowed to remove it *for five hours!* His wife was rudely forced into her room, his sister, Mrs. Thomas, denied admittance to the house; but finally obtaining it, was insulted, and the proposal made in her hearing, to cut the body "into bits." Even when the sorrow of his family was venting itself in tears and lamentations, some monster shouted to them to "stop their howling!" They robbed the corpse of the keys and money which were in the pocket. They ordered the family to leave the house and carry the corpse with them, before 5 o'clock, threatening to cast it into the street if they did not, and it was with difficulty the mayor and citizens of the town could persuade them to extend the time till the next morning at day-break. On leaving in the morning, the hack and hearse were frequently stopped, and the most inhuman insults heaped on the family by wretches who thrust their heads through the hack windows, and the fearful threats of whom stifled with choking agony the grief of the wife, the daughter, the sister.

Note No. 4—Page 39.—Amelia, Alice, and Caroline, are the names of these most interesting little girls. The family of Jackson has received universally the sympathy of the South, which has expressed that sympathy not only in word, but in liberal donations for their benefit. It may be well to state, however, that the loss they have sustained, not only by the violent death of the husband and father, but in the deprivation of a home, deserves a continuance of these charities. The furniture of the Marshall House had been purchased by Jackson for $7,000, and his wife has now that debt also to pay, unless it shall be otherwise liquidated.

Note No. 5—Page 40.—Since writing the foregoing we have learned that the mother of Jackson has been "gallantly captured" by a crowd of Yankee soldiers. Suspecting that she had been sending food to our pickets in her neighborhood, relying for their belief on the testimony of one of her run-away negroes, a party went to her house one night and tried to entrap her by passing for Southern troops. She discovered their treachery, and told them in plain terms what she thought of them. A few days after they took her prisoner, and forced her, though sixty-seven years old, to walk several miles before they would get a carriage for her. At the same time they took Mr. Moore, an old gentleman, her half brother, and Mrs. Stewart, her daughter. They are now in one of the Washington prisons. They took all her negroes which could be of service to them, and gave the others away. They destroyed her furniture, and appropriated a quantity of house-keeping stores which she had laid up.

NOTE No. 6—Page 41.—The respect and admiration the people have for the memory of Jackson have been shown from the moment his death was known. When the corpse arrived at Fairfax Court House, the bell at the Court House was tolled, and the citizens and soldiers en masse went out to receive the cortege, and meeting it about a mile from the village, lined the road on both sides, and with uncovered heads, suffered it to pass through their lines, then followed on in solemn procession.

When it arrived at his mother's, the place of burial, a large crowd had gathered to receive it. The grief of his eldest daughter there broke forth in most pitiable vehemence. She raised the head from the coffin, which was opened at her request, and embracing it and uttering the most pathetic entreaties, was with difficulty removed. The services were performed, in the absence of a regular minister, by Mr. George W. Gunnell, an old church-elder of the neighborhood. When he had finished, he raised his hands, and gazing into the grave, earnestly exclaimed, "Would to God it were my son!" The old gentleman has since been imprisoned by the Lincoln minions.

We append a selection from the many verses in which Jackson's deed has been celebrated. The first is by M. B. Wharton, of South Carolina, and is entitled

STAND BY YOUR FLAG.

Stand by your flag ye Southern braves,
Ye hold it as fair freedom's trust;
Swear that it e'er in triumph waves,
Or else you'll with it kiss the dust.
'Tis yours by every sacred tie
Of honor, valor, interest, birth;
The hopes of millions 'neath it lie,
The bravest and the best of earth.

Stand by your flag as Jackson stood,
  Who let the tyrant's minions know
That when it fell, his own life blood
  In its defence should freely flow;
That if they would invasion make
  He would *alone* begin the fray,
And for each inch he dared to take
  At least an *Ells-worth* they should pay.

He loved his flag and wished it saved.
  He prized the beauties that it wore.
Near Vernon's sleeping Chief it waved,
  His house the name of Marshall bore!
And hark, the sound of fife and drum!
  In glittering files behold the foe!
With shouts and threat'ning cries they come,
  They halt with menaces below.

"Down with your flag!" the spoilers cry.
  Oh. how his brave pulsations bound!
Did he obey? His shots reply—
  He brings his foeman to the ground.
But he fell too. For country's sake,
  He on her altar bleeding lies;
He sleeps in realms of bliss to wake,
  For God accepts the sacrifice.

———

The other is by 'T. F., Augusta, Ga.

JACKSON, OUR FIRST MARTYR.

Not where the battle red
Covers with fame the dead;
Not where the trumpet calls
Vengeance for each that falls;
Not with his comrade dear,
Not there he fell—not there.

He grasps no brother's hand,
He sees no patriot band;
Daring alone the foe,
He strikes, then waits the blow;
Counting his life not dear,
His was no heart to fear.

Shout, shout his deed of glory,
Tell it in song and story;

Tell it where soldiers brave
Rush fearless to the grave ?
Tell it—a magic spell
In that great deed shall dwell.

Yes, he hath won a name
Deathless for age to fame ;
Our Flag, baptised in blood,
Away, as with a flood,
Shall sweep the tyrant band
Whose feet pollute our land.

His martyr-patriot fall
Shall be a trumpet call
For all true men to go
To crush the invading foe.
Let not his blood in vain
Cry from the soil they stain.

Then Freemen raise the cry,
As Freemen live or die.
Arm, arm you for the fight,
His banner in your sight—
And this your battle-cry,
"*Jackson and Victory !*"

The following is the card published by Jackson on leasing the Marshall House :

MARSHALL HOUSE—JAMES W. JACKSON, PROPRIETOR.

Corner King and Pitt Streets, Alexandria, Va.

Virginia is determined, and will yet conquer under the command of JEFF. DAVIS.

We append as a most touching incident connected with this history, the following copies of newspaper slips found in Jackson's pocket after his death, and kindly furnished us by his niece, who found them, and whom we are glad to number among the most agreeable and interesting of our young friends.

This young lady has preserved them just as he tore them from the newspapers, and they tell a story of the devotion and determination of the man which no language can improve.

LAND OF THE SOUTH.

BY A. F. LEONARD.

Land of the South! the fairest land
Beneath Columbia's sky!
Proudly her hills of freedom stand,
Her plains in beauty lie.
Her dotted fields, her traversed streams
Their annual wealth renew.
Land of the South! in brightest dreams
No dearer spot we view.

Men of the South! A free-born race,
They vouch a patriot line;
Ready the foeman's van to face,
And guard their Country's shrine.
By sire and son a haloing light
Through time is borne along;
They "nothing ask but what is right,"
And *will* not suffer wrong!

———

"Many a mother's heart shall mourn her long lament over the lifeless, form of a son who shed his blood upon an ensanguined field. Many a wife's wail of sorrow shall be heard for a husband torn by death's ruthless hand from her bosom. But mother, wife, your sons and husbands could die in no nobler cause than in defence of their homes. Their names will be written with an iron pen on the scroll of fame, having sacrificed their lives on the altar of Liberty. Bards shall sing in heroic verse of their deeds and sufferings, and they will be handed down to future generations, as noble examples of devotion to their country."

www.ingramcontent.com/pod-product-compliance
Lightning Source LLC
Chambersburg PA
CBHW030910260626
47169CB00008B/2773